Climb up a **Mountain**

by Dana Meachen Rau

Photographs by Romie Flanagan

THE ROURKE PRESS
Vero Beach, Florida

For Chris and our trips up Wheeler.

—D. M. R.

Thanks to the Becton-Martin family
for providing the modeling for this book.

Photographs ©: Flanagan Publishing Services/Romie Flanagan

An Editorial Directions Book

Book design and production by Ox and Company

Library of Congress Cataloging-in-Publication Data

Rau, Dana Meachen, 1971-
    Climb up a mountain / Dana Meachen Rau.
        p. cm. — (The adventurers)
    Includes index.
    Summary: Climbing a mountain involves seeing slithering snakes, reading a
map, and watching a sunset from the summit.
        ISBN 1-57103-317-3
        [1. Mountaineering—Fiction.] I. Title.

PZ7.R193975 C1 2000   99-086667
[E]—dc21
© 2001 The Rourke Press, Inc.

Printed in the United States of America.

Are you ready for an adventure?

There are many things to see and do when you climb up a mountain!

Gear bag.

Binoculars.

Compass.

That's what I *wear* when
I climb up a mountain.

Big rocks.

Mountain goats.

Spiky trees.

That's what I *see* when
I climb up a mountain.

Read a map.

Follow directions.

Look down below.

That's what I *do* when
I climb up a mountain.

More Information about Mountains

A mountain is a landform that is higher than the land around it. Some mountains stand alone. Some are part of a group called a range. Mountains are made by movements of the earth or by volcanoes. Mountains are found on all seven continents.

To Find Out More about Your Environment

Books

Landau, Elaine. *Mountain Animals.* Danbury, Conn.: Children's Press, 1996.

Parker, Steve. *Mountains.* Danbury, Conn.: Franklin Watts, 1998.

Taylor, Barbara. *Mountains and Volcanoes.* New York: Kingfisher Books, 1993.

Web Sites

America's Roof
http://www.americasroof.com/usa.shtml
This site is devoted to the highest places in the world.

The Evergreen Project Adventures
http://mbgnet.mobot.org
This site is devoted to teaching kids about environments.

About the Author

When Dana Meachen Rau was a child, she and her mother often walked in the woods and splashed in ponds to find the creatures hiding there. Dana loved to write down her thoughts and draw pictures to remember her outdoor adventures. Today, Dana is a children's book editor and illustrator and has authored more than thirty books for children. She takes adventures with her husband, Chris, and son, Charlie, in Farmington, Connecticut.